The Three Princes

Written by Berlie Doherty
Illustrated by Cosei Kawa

Collins

A long time ago, and far, far away, there were
three princes. They were so alike that only their mother
could tell them apart. When she died, it seemed that
no one would ever know for sure who was who,
especially as each of the princes loved to pretend
he was one of the others.

And as for their father, he never knew anyway.
Sometimes he thought that Raman was the vainest, and
Emir was the most athletic, and Salman was the funniest.

But sometimes it would be Raman who would run like the wind, with sand spraying round his feet, and Salman who would dress himself up like a peacock, and Emir, swift-footed Emir, who would just tell jokes and lounge about all day on silk cushions. To make things easier for himself, the sultan just called each of them, "My son".

On their 16th birthday, he decided it was time to introduce the princes to some of the noble families in Arabia. He would look foolish if he didn't even know their names. He called them to his high chamber, and asked them to tell him truthfully which one was which.

"Make sure you tell me the truth, my sons," he said, "because one day it'll be very important."

And they solemnly told him.

"I'm Raman," said Raman, and his father slipped
a ruby ring on to his finger. It glowed like the juice of
a pomegranate.

"I'm Salman," said Salman, and he was
given a sapphire ring that flashed like
the colours of the sea.

"And you must be Emir, my son,"
the sultan said to the third one.

"I've bought you an emerald
ring. Green as the grass that follows
the desert rains. Now people will
always know which of you is which.
Go out into the world, and find
yourselves a beautiful princess to marry."

And so it was that the three princes arrived at
the gorgeous palace of the sultan of Byzantium. He had
a beautiful daughter called Halima, who had skin as soft
as peaches, hair the colour of blackbirds' wings and
eyes like drops of honey. They all fell in love with her
at first sight. Just like that. Like magic.

The three princes stayed at the sultan's palace for
a whole month, and Princess Halima raced with them
on the sultan's famous black horses, visited bazaars with
them on grumbling camels and danced with them in
the marbled halls of her father's palace.

And all this time, she was never quite sure who was who because they were always swapping rings, just to tease her. Raman loves sweets best, she thought. And Emir is always falling off his camel, and Salman has the nicest smile, but as soon as she told them that she knew for sure which was which, they swapped rings again, and Raman would only eat apricots, and Emir would ride his camel as skilfully as a circus entertainer, and Salman would scowl as if he had a mouthful of lemon juice.

But one day, Princess Halima fell in love with one of them.

It happened on her birthday. On that day she wore a new gown that was the colour of mulberries. She'd never looked more beautiful. One by one the princes lost their hearts to her.

Raman met her by the fountain, and they both got showered with water and ran away from each other, shrieking with laughter.

8

Salman took her out to see the stars, and they both lay on their backs and looked up at the enormous sky and the stars like petals falling.

And Emir shared an orange with her while he told her a story about a city built into rock that was the colour of roses. Her eyes were round with wonder as he told it, and he was so enchanted by her beauty that he fell in love with her, there and then. And she fell in love with him.

That day, the day of her birthday, the sultan called Princess Halima to his throne room. He told her that he had decided that it was time for her to marry, and that he was sending his courtiers far and wide to find a suitable husband for her.

"But you don't have to look far, Father," she said. "I know who I want to marry. I'm already in love."

"Well, that makes things easier," her father agreed. "What's his name?"

The princess looked puzzled then. "Well, it's Emir, I think. Or it might be Salman. Or it might be Raman."

The father sent for the princes. All three went down on their knees.

"My daughter wishes to marry one of you," he said.

"Yes, we'd like to marry your daughter," they all said.

"Which one did you say you loved?" the sultan asked Princess Halima.

"I'm not sure," she said. "I thought I knew ..."

"Well, you can't marry all three of them, that's for sure."
Her father was getting impatient.

"Perhaps they could do some tricks for her,"
the grand vizier said helpfully.

Princess Halima looked at Raman, and he did a few wonderful somersaults across the floor, that made everyone gasp and clap with joy. But then she looked at Salman, and he played his flute so beautifully that a snake uncoiled from a basket and swayed like a dreamy dancer, and again everyone clapped and gasped. Emir juggled with two, four, eight, no, 16 oranges.

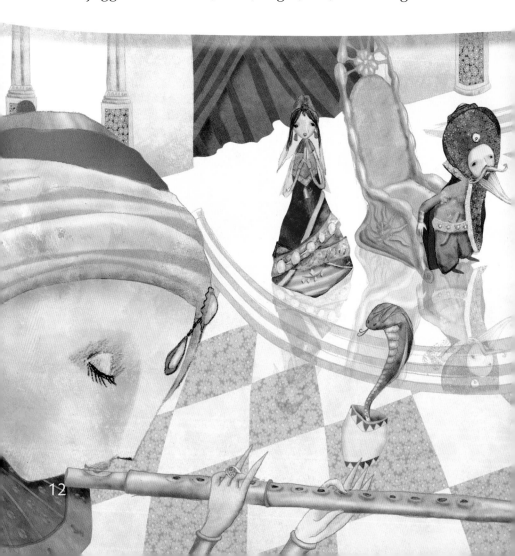

"Wonderful!" everyone said.

It was no good. She couldn't tell one from the other any more.

Her father sighed. "I like you all," he said. "I'd be quite happy for any of you to be my son-in-law. But only one of you can marry my daughter."

"May I make another suggestion," the grand vizier said, and he mumbled into the sultan's ear while the princess smiled at the princes and they smiled back at her.

At last the sultan spoke. "I'm going to send all three of you away. The first one to come back with something beautiful and magical to give my daughter will be the one to marry her. Now go."

14

So the three brothers saddled their
camels and set off across the desert to
find something wonderful and magical to give
to the princess Halima.

After three days of travelling the princes agreed
to split up, and to meet together at the same place
when the moon was full again. They travelled far and
wide across the dry rivers and desert plains, they
survived fizzy sand storms whipped up by wind, they
were thirsty and hungry, but at last, when the moon
was full, they came together.

"I have the perfect gift!" said Raman, even before his brothers had reached him. "I met an old man in a golden cloak, and he gave me this mirror, look!" He drew out of his camel's bag a beautiful mirror, crusted with emeralds, topaz, amber and ruby. He gazed into it lovingly.

"It's very beautiful," Salman and Emir agreed. "But is it magical?"

"Oh yes," Raman said. "The old man told me that sometimes, only sometimes, you can look into it and see something that's happening far, far away. Not now, of course, but sometimes," he added anxiously. "All he wanted for it was my ring."

"Well," said Salman, "I met an old man in a silver cloak, and he gave me this carpet, in exchange for my ring."

He slid a roll of carpet from his camel's back and shook it out in front of them. "Look at the wonderful colours in it! Look at the beautiful silk tassels, like camels' eyelashes! She'll love it. Oh, and it's magical all right," he added. "It's a flying carpet. Princess Halima can sit on it and travel anywhere in the world."

"I met a man who was dressed in rags," Emir said,
"and I gave him my ring so he could buy himself
a cloak. And he gave me this." He produced an orange.
"It was all he had."

"An orange? What's beautiful about that?"

"It's round and golden, like the sun." Prince Emir threw it in the air and caught it again. "And anyway, Princess Halima loves oranges," he said.

"And what's magical about it?"

"I don't know," Emir said.

Raman and Salman smiled at each other over Emir's head.

Later that night the three princes looked into the mirror.
For a moment they could see nothing in it except their
own faces, but then a mist fell across it and cleared again.
Then the mirror showed them a scene that filled them
with horror. They saw Princess Halima lying on her bed,
pale and listless, her eyes closed tight. Her father was
kneeling by her, his hands across his face. As they looked,
the court physician came into the chamber and took
the princess's hand.

"She's ill," they heard him say. "I'm afraid she's dying."

"Oh no!" the brothers cried. "And we're so far away from her. We must go to her at once."

"My carpet will take us to her," Salman said. "Sit on it, quickly. Hold tight!"

The carpet brought them instantly to the sultan's palace, right inside Princess Halima's chamber.

"She's thirsty," the court physician was saying.

"Water!" shouted Raman, jumping up and down. He held up his mirror to see if he could find some reflected there.

"I'll get it," shouted Salman, tripping over his carpet in his haste to get some.

"My orange!" said Emir. Trembling, he peeled the orange
and broke off a segment. He squeezed it against
the princess's mouth, so the golden juice trickled
between her lips. She opened her eyes, and sat up.
She looked round, puzzled to see so many people
weeping by her bed.

"Have I been sleeping?" she asked.

"You've been dying," her father said. "But now, magic of
magic, you're better!"

"You were very ill," said the court physician. "But you
were better as soon as you tasted the orange.
How strange!"

"It was my orange! My orange!" Emir shouted.

He pulled the segments apart, and ran round the room giving one to each of his brothers, one to the sultan, to the physician, to the grand vizier, to the nurses, to the courtiers, till there was nothing left of it for him. "My orange cured you!" he said happily. "It saved your life! What a beautiful, magical gift!"

"But without my magic mirror, we'd never have known she was ill," said Raman. "My gift is the most magical."

"No, without my magic carpet, we'd never have got here in time to save her," said Salman. "My gift is the most magical."

"The princess must choose," said the grand vizier, stepping forward.

The three princes stared at him.

"You look just like the old man in the golden cloak, who gave me my mirror in exchange for my ring," said Raman.

"But you're just like the old man in the silver cloak, who gave me my carpet in exchange for *my* ring," said Salman.

"Ah, but you look like the poor old man in rags I gave my ring to. The one who gave me the orange," said Emir.

"Which just goes to show", said the grand vizier, "that however many times one person changes his appearance, he's still the same inside. Raman and Salman thought of themselves, whilst Emir thought of the poor man who had nothing. His was a selfless act, and this is what he's like, no matter what ring he wears."

"Hmm," said the sultan, scratching his turban. "But we still don't know which one my daughter is to marry!"

"I know." Princess Halima went to her father, stood on tiptoe and whispered in his ear. "I know exactly who is who. Raman gave me a beautiful mirror, but he's very vain. I think he chose it because he likes to look at himself in it! And Salman gave me a carpet, and it's gorgeous, I know, but I think he chose it because he's a bit showy himself. But Emir knows I love oranges!" She went over to Emir and stood next to him. "This is the one I want to marry. I knew him as soon as I awoke. He smelt of oranges, and it reminded me of the day I fell in love with him. Even though he doesn't have his emerald ring any more, I know it's Emir, and I love him."

The sultan placed Princess Halima's hand into Prince Emir's. "Then you shall be married," he said. "Salman, Raman and Emir, thank you, you all brought wonderful gifts for my daughter. Salman and Raman, you may keep your mirror and your carpet for ever, and may they help you to find true wives.

Emir's orange has all gone, but he has already given my daughter something wonderful – love. True love is the most magical gift of all."

Three magical gifts

31

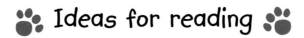

Ideas for reading

Written by Linda Pagett B.Ed (hons), M.Ed
Lecturer and Educational Consultant

Reading objectives:
- predict what might happen from details stated and implied
- ask questions to improve their understanding of a text
- draw inferences such as inferring characters' feelings, thoughts and motives
- identify themes and conventions in a wide range of books

Spoken language objectives:
- use spoken language to develop understanding

- give well-structured descriptions, explanations and narratives for different purposes
- maintain attention and participate actively in collaborative conversations

Curriculum links: Citizenship

Interest words: amber, bazaar, Byzantium, emerald, mulberries, pomegranate, ruby, sapphire, selfless, somersault, sultan, topaz, vizier

Resources: writing materials

Build a context for reading

This book can be read over two or more reading sessions.

- Read the blurb and look at the front cover together. Discuss ideas for what the magical object referred to in the blurb could be.

- Ask children which country they think the story may be set in. What clues are there on the cover to suggest this?

- Ask children to name other traditional tales that they know. Do any of them refer to three things, e.g. three wishes, three daughters?

Understand and apply reading strategies

- Read up to p5 together and ask children to predict what they think might happen next, making a note of their ideas.

- Ask children to read to p7 silently and discuss in pairs the characters of the three princes, prompting them with questions if necessary, e.g. *Why do the princes keep changing their identities?*

- Ask children to read to p19, and as a group discuss their predictions for the end of the book. Which magical gift do they think will win the princess's heart, and why?

- Direct children to read silently to the end, making a note of which predictions were correct and which were not.